Little Raccoon Takes Charge

By Lilian Moore
Illustrated by Deborah Borgo

Adapted from LITTLE RACCOON AND NO TROUBLE AT ALL

A GOLDEN BOOK • NEW YORK
Western Publishing Company, Inc., Racine, Wisconsin 53404

Copyright © 1986 by Lilian Moore. Illustrations copyright © 1986 by Deborah Borgo. All rights reserved. Printed in the U.S.A. by Western Publishing Company, Inc. No part of this book may be reproduced or copied in any form without written permission from the publisher. GOLDEN®, GOLDEN & DESIGN®, A GOLDEN BOOK®, and A BIG LITTLE GOLDEN BOOK® are trademarks of Western Publishing Company, Inc. Library of Congress Catalog Card Number: 85-51679
ISBN 0-307-10254-8/ISBN 0-307-68254-4 (lib. bdg.) B C D E F G H I J

"Little Raccoon," said his mother,
"Mother Chipmunk and I must go out today.
Will you take care of her two baby
chipmunks till we get back?"

Little Raccoon looked at the
baby chipmunks.

"I never did *that* before," he said.

The two chipmunks sat very still.
   "See how good they are,"
said Mother Chipmunk.
"They will be no trouble at all."
   So little. So good.
And no trouble at all.
   "All right," said Little Raccoon.
"I will take care of them."

Mother Chipmunk thanked him.
So did Mother Raccoon.
Then they went away.
Little Raccoon looked at the chipmunks.
"He's my brother," said one.
"She's my sister," said the other.

"Play with us," said the brother.

"Play *follow me*," said the sister.

"I never did that before,"
said Little Raccoon.

"All you do is follow us,"
said the brother.

The chipmunks ran to a tree.
   "Follow us!" they cried.
And they ran up the tree.
   So Little Raccoon ran up the tree, too.
   The chipmunks ran out on a branch.
Whoosh! They jumped into the next tree.
   "Follow us!" they cried.

So Little Raccoon ran out
on the branch, too.
But the branch was too small for him.
Crash!
He came tumbling down.

The chipmunks ran to the old stone wall.
There was a hole in the wall,
and they ran inside.
"Come in!" they called. "Follow us!"
Little Raccoon picked himself up.
"This game is hard work," he thought.

Little Raccoon stuck his head and
front paws into the hole in the wall.
But the hole was too small for him.
"I can't get in," he cried.
"And I can't get out!"
The chipmunks laughed.
"Little Raccoon is stuck!"

Little Raccoon began to wiggle.
At last with a big wiggle
he came tumbling out.
    The chipmunks came running
out of the hole.
    "Here we are!" they cried.
    "No more games!" said Little Raccoon.
The chipmunks sat very still.

"We know a good trick," said the sister.
"A trick?" said Little Raccoon. "Show me!"
The chipmunks ran and hid behind a tree.
"Try to find us," they called.
"That's easy," said Little Raccoon,
and he ran around the tree.
But the chipmunks went faster.

Little Raccoon ran fast, but the
chipmunks went faster and faster.
Little Raccoon got so dizzy
he had to sit down.
"Here we are!" cried the chipmunks.
"No more tricks!" said Little Raccoon.
The chipmunks sat very still.

"I'm hungry!" said the sister.
"So am I!" said the brother.
"And so am I!" thought Little Raccoon.
"Do you like crayfish?" he asked.
"We like butternuts," said the brother.
"And beechnuts," said the sister.
"What's crayfish?"

"It's the best of all,"
said Little Raccoon.
"Let's go to the running stream
and get some."
The chipmunks jumped up.
"Stay right behind me,"
said Little Raccoon. And off they went.

On the way, Little Raccoon thought
happily about crayfish.
Suddenly something hit him
on the head. Once. Then again.
"Here we are!" the chipmunks called
from a butternut tree.
"Stop that!" cried Little Raccoon.
"And come right down!"

The chipmunks came running down
from the tree.
   "I must think of *something*
to make them behave,"
thought Little Raccoon.
But all he said was,
"Follow me."

Up the stream was the beaver pond.
In the middle of the pond
Beaver was working.
When Little Raccoon saw Beaver,
he had an idea.

"Watch me," he called to the chipmunks.
They saw him catch a fat crayfish.
They saw him swim to Beaver's house.

They watched Little Raccoon sitting there, eating crayfish.

"This crayfish is *so* good," he called to the chipmunks.

"We want some," they cried. "Take us there."

"Hop on my tail," said Beaver, and he took them across.

Little Raccoon gave them some crayfish.
Then he swam back across the pond
and began to fish.

"We don't like crayfish,"
called the brother.

"We don't like it here,"
said the sister.

Little Raccoon just went on fishing.

"We want to go home!" cried the chipmunks.

"No more games?" said Little Raccoon.
"No more tricks?
No more tree fun?"

"Oh, no!" said the chipmunks.

So Beaver took them back
across the pond.

"Stay right behind me,"
said Little Raccoon.
"All the way home!"
    That's what the chipmunks did.
They got home just as Mother Raccoon
and Mother Chipmunk walked in.

"Hello, my little ones,"
said Mother Chipmunk. "Were you good?
Were they good, Little Raccoon?"

The chipmunks looked
at Little Raccoon.
Little Raccoon looked
at the chipmunks.
"No trouble at all,"
said Little Raccoon.